BLAST-OFF BALCONY

REAL FAIRYVERSITY

Gwendolyn
Becomes a Real Tooth Fairy

As Told by The Real Tooth Fairies to
Rachel E. Frankel

Fairy Portraits by A-M Basom
Stepella & Furry Portraits by Kelly Grupczynski

Book 4

Be a Beauty Inside!

On a magical morning in Real Fairyland, fairies woke up in their floating beds, fluffed their wings, and powered up their wands with Glow. But this day was especially fabberful - it was a new school year at Real Fairyversity!

Gwendolyn fairy was especially excited and nervous. Her family was one of the most famous in Real Fairyland. For generations, her ancestors had served on the High Royal Council and attended Royal Balls with her Highness, Fairy Queen Sirona.

But Gwendolyn never spent much time with fairy girls. She grew up studying in her grand villa with private tutors and her personal attendant, Fleur. Finally, this year she would go to school with other fairies!

Inside Gwendolyn's fashion closet, Fleur asked, "Want to wear this for your first day, Gwennie?"

"Or maybe this laughing gown?" Fleur giggled as she held a magic laugh ribbon. Gwennie smiled, "Hm, maybe not my first day. Oh, I hope the fairies like me!"

Gwendolyn's pet Furry, Rosie, wanted her to feel confident today so Rosie mixed up a perfume called "Be Yoursmellf." POOF! "Oh, Rosie, it's scent-sational!" Gwendolyn said.

Be Your Smellf

Gwennie chose a poppin' pink dress and flew off to school. Rosie squeaked, "Just be yoursmellf, Gwennie!"

4

At school, fairies and elffs were inviting friends to join school clubs. "Join the Spy Spells Club!" a fairy called. One said, "Join Marching Band and launch spells from your flute!"

Then Gwennie heard a voice screech, "Buy a cookie bag and everyone will like you!" Gwennie said, "Perfect," handing over 10 Sparkle dollars. But when she opened the bag, only a dot was inside!

REAL FAIRYVERSITY

SPY SPELLS CLUB

MAGIC MARCHING BAND

stepella's prank stand

"I polka-dotchoo-gotchoo!" Stepella laughed. "This is the Pranks Club, dearie!" I said it was a cookie BAG, not cookies, ha-ha!" Gwendolyn muttered, "Hm, I don't think I'll be joining this club!"

Schedule
9:00 Fashion
10:00 Potionometry

REAL FAIRYVERSITY

Flying inside, a butterfly dropped a schedule in Gwendolyn's hand. "My first class is Fairy Fashions!" Gwennie's designs had already won medals at the Flying Couture Awards. She flew into class and sat by two smiling fairies. She said, "Hi! I'm Gwendolyn."

FAIRY CAM
Fairy Wing Trends
High-Flying Style!

Class Rules
✦ Raise your wands to speak.
✦ No flying bubblegum bubbles!
✦ No spell-casting on the teacher.
Miss ZeZe

MODA FAIRY

One of the fairies answered, "Hi! I'm Adriana and this is Kimora. You're new, huh?" Gwennie smiled, "I am! It's great to meet you fairies. And I'm super excited for Fairy Fashion cl . . ." "AHEM!" an irritated voice interrupted.

Gwendolyn turned to see a fairy sneering at her.

"*D*o you know where you're sitting?" the fairy demanded. Gwennie uttered, "In design class?" The fairy snapped, "Umm, NO! You're in MY seat! So flutter away!"

*G*wendolyn got up shocked. The fairy added, "I know who you are, Gwendolyn. Just because you win silly dress awards and have private tutors, doesn't mean you're going to rule BABETTE'S world!"

*G*wennie scooped up her things in such a flurry that she accidentally knocked over Babette's design portfolio!

"*Yipes!* You bent MY portfolio!
Flying flops!" Then Babette squealed
at Adriana and Kimora,
" Help me NOW, fairies!"

Adriana and Kimora
obediently rushed to
Babette's side. Adriana
said, "We'll help you,
Babette! Who does that
new girl think she is?"
Kimora added, "We all
know YOU are the
best designer at Real
Fairyversity!"

All Gwennie could do
was sink into her new desk
and hold back crystal tears.
Why were these fairies
being so unkind?

Gwendolyn tried to focus on the Fairy Cam announcements. It was Twinkle, the Real Tooth Fairies leader. "Welcome back to another magical school year at Real Fairyversity! First, look out for a case of flying hiccups going around. If you see fairies flippity-flying, use this spell:

Wippity-wappity, yippity-yow!
Flippity hic-cups, zip away now!

"In other news," Twinkle continued, "there's a fabberful Fashion Show tomorrow. If you'd like to participate, call the show's director, Babette, on her Wand-a-phone. Have a Glowy day, fairies and remember to spread kindness!"

"Oh, no! Babette's directing the fashion show," sighed Gwennie. "Making new friends may be harder than I thought!"

The rest of the morning went by in a whirlwind of hiccups and unknown faces. By lunchtime, Gwennie looked in her locker and thought, "I should just zap away these books, and give up on Fairyversity! I miss Fleur and my tutors!"

Magi-Matics

But Gwennie's fairy heart wouldn't let her give up. She mustered a smile and saw an empty floating table in the lunch courtyard.

She flew to grab a lunch balloon and a cup at Frosty Fountain, thinking, "Surely some friendly fairies will come and sit with me."

Just then a voice said, "AHEM! Well, lookity look who's in MY lunch seat! This is MY table for MY friends." Oh no! Gwennie didn't have the courage to answer Babette. She grabbed her Starry Smoothie and sadly flew away.

As she left, she heard Adriana say, "Babette, give her a break!" Kimora added, "She does have style. Check out her stilettos!" Babette just snapped, "Oh, ugh, whatever!" but she did steal a glance at Gwendolyn's shoes.

BLAST-OFF BALCONY

Gwennie had lost her appetite. She threw away her singing sandwich and wandered onto the balcony.

She sighed, "Everyone has friends but me." She accidentally leaned on the GO button of the Blast-Off Balcony! Away she flew!

"When the Going Gets Tough, the Tough Get Glowing!"

PART 2

A Dreamy
Afternoon

The balcony flew Gwendolyn to a castle tower with tiny trees as high as the eye could see. But these were no ordinary trees! Each tree was in a vase with a portrait of an Earthie. It had branches for talents, dreams, and kindness.

Swennie flew to the trees for a closer look. "Wow! This tree belongs to an Earthie girl named Ashley." There on Ashley's dream branch was a wish for a poppin' pink party dress. Gwendolyn forgot her problems and blurted out, "How amazical! I designed a dress just like that!"

My Future Dreams

Kindness I Did

Gave Flowers

My Now Dreams

Kindness Done for Me

Gold Medal

Dream

I ♥ U

My Talents

My Achievements

Dad Helped Me

Dress

SINGING

READING CHAMP

DUNK IT!

Made the Team

Eat junk food

Ickies

Ashley

Dream

Dress

"Well, hello, fairy. What are you doing in the Tower of Dreams?" asked a voice behind Gwendolyn. "Oh no!" she sighed. "I must be in some other fairy's way!" But then she saw four smiling faces.

She breathed easier and answered, "Oh, starrily sorry! I'm Gwennie and my first day at Real Fairyversity hasn't been easy. Then I accidentally took off in the Blast-Off Balcony and landed here!"

"I'm Avalanne," the fairy replied. "And these are my friends, Triana, Brigitte and Stacey."

"It's fabberful to fly into such friendly fairies," Gwennie smiled. "What is this place and who is that fashionable Earthie Ashley?"

"She's splendi-doodley sweet too," Triana said. "This is her Real Dream Tree where I put her lost teeth to help her dreams come true." Brigitte added, "All of us Real Tooth Fairies love helping Earthies' Real Dream Trees grow and Glow!"

"Wow, you're Real Tooth Fairies!" Gwendolyn said. "I read about kindness you do in the Real Fairyland News. And I saw Twinkle on the announcements at Fairyversity today!"

14

"Don't you love Twinkle!" Stacey said. "She's leader of the Real Tooth Fairies. And as for Ashley, she wants to give this party dress to her sister as a birthday present. You see, her dad lost his job, so they can't afford it."

"Oh my curls!" Gwendolyn said. "I wish there was some way I could help!"

"That's amazically kind of you, Gwendolyn," Avalanne said. "Follow us - there's something special we want to show you!"

PRESENT·POPPER
A Tassel for Ashley

TOOTH RECORDS

The fairies arrived at a bustling castle tower, where Gwennie was in awe. "This is Surprises Central," Triana explained, "where we gather presents and Magic Letters to bring to Earthies like Ashley." Gwendolyn said, "It's just awesomous! I want to see how it all works!"

SURPRISES CENTRAL

"Tee-hee," Brigitte giggled. "Maybe later. But for now, you'd better be getting back to Fairyversity." Gwennie glided to her next class with her new friends, giggling and chatting as they flew over Real Fairyland.

When Gwendolyn saw Babette in Potionometry, her heart sank. But then she saw Professor Spellbeaker's fun assignment!

"Perfect!" Gwendolyn thought. "THIS I can do!" She was an ace in Make-Over Magic. Gwennie read in her chemistry book and planned her mixture, using the laws of science and advanced fairy magic.

CHOCOLATE YUM

Shine

FAIRY CHEM

ROCK'N BEAT

GLOW

CAN'T RESIST

Yum

Gwendolyn was about to try on her creation when Adriana swished some on her lips. "Wow, Gwennie! This is yummy and it makes me want to dance! What is it?"

Spell-ing Bee
Show your newest spell!

Gwennie said, "It's my Chocolate-Rock-It Lip Gloss. I love doing new Make-Over Magic formulas!" Adriana was about to say, "Me too," when she saw Babette glare at them. "Oh," Adriana whispered. "I'd better get back to Babette. Fly by you later!"

Gwennie was packing up after class when who should bump into her floating chemistry book? "Oh, soooo sorry," Babette said, faking a smile. "How could I be SO clumsy?" She flipped her hair and flew off.

*S*tepella the pranking Whatsie peeked in and said, "Now there's someone you need to prank, Miss Gwennie-Penny! I could sell you my Monkey Breath cookie to give her, or my Stuck-On-You Bath Soap. It'll cover her with dots all day!"

*G*wennie managed a laugh as she fluttered away. "No pranks for me now, thanks!" Gwennie was tired from her topsy-turvy first day at school. Before flying home, though, there was one more thing she wanted to do.

Gwendolyn tip-toed back into the Tower of Dreams. Pulling a magic ribbon from her wand, she pointed at Ashley's Real Dream Tree and chanted a spell. The dress on Ashley's tree became real!

POOF!

With another wave of her wand, Gwennie wrapped the dress for Ashley to give to her sister.

She set it under Ashley's Real Dream Tree and said, "I hope my surprise makes this Earthie happy! I'm sure Triana will find it and take it to Ashley." Little did Gwendolyn know that Twinkle was right there seeing her act of kindness!

Be a Beauty Inside!

The next day, Fleur and Rosie could see Gwennie was looking sad. Rosie nuzzled her nose into Gwennie's neck and hugged her. "Thanks, Rosie!" Gwennie smiled. "New things can be hard but I'm sure it'll get better each day!"

MODA FAIRY

"That's the way to Glow, Gwennie!" Fleur said. Gwendolyn was filled with poppin' positivity as she flew off to school.

REAL FAIRYVERSITY

ELFF INSTITUTE of TIME TRAVEL

"When you least expect it, love works its magic!"

PART 3

A Fairy
Fashion Glow

Gwennie's day began with Magimatics class. Then she sat with the Real Tooth Fairies at lunch! By Potionometry, Gwendolyn felt ready for anything. To her surprise, Babette smiled and said, "Gwensie, we got off on the wrong wing yesterday. I'd be super excited if you'd design dresses for the fashion show today."

Babette batted her wings and eyelashes, looking as innocent as can be. "Oh, I'd love to!" answered Gwennie. "Perrrrfect!" Babette said. "See you at the Flying Divas Fashion Runway, Gwensie!"

Stepella peeked around the corner, "Ya shoulda told her, 'No way, Fake-o-Babettesy!' " Gwen giggled, "No pranks now, Stepella!"

Divas With Wings Fashion Show

After school, Gwendolyn fluttered onto the Fashion Runway. Near the stage, fairies were flying around getting dresses ready for the show.

"Oh, Gwensie-pie! You're here," said Babette. "You can start designing dresses for Adriana and Kimora." On the runway, Gwendolyn saw some of the Real Tooth Fairies. "Are they in the Fashion Show too?" she asked. "Well, duh!" Babette answered. "Every fairy who's any fairy will be here! Come along, Adriana, Gwennie will do your dress first!"

Gwennie thought for a second and began her Make-Over Magic for Adriana.

"Beautiful beads of Pink and blue! A shimmery gorgeous gown for you!" POOF!

Ribbons swirled around Adriana to create a jeweled gown. "Wow! I lusciously love it, Gwennie!" Adriana gushed.

"My, you've outdone yourself this time, Gwensicle," Babette said, forcing the compliment. "Next! Kimora!" Babette smirked as she sneaked up to stand behind Kimora.

Then Gwennie began her spell:
"Red and purple all aglow,
A gown for you in the Fashion Show!"
POOF!

A cascade of ribbon wrapped around Kimora, but something was wrong. The ribbon revealed a beautiful dress, but there were black spots on it!

*"A*hh! SPIDERS!" Kimora yelled out. Gwennie did an instant Repel Spell as the spiders crawled away. "Gwendolyn, what a nasty trick you did!" Babette sneered as she comforted Kimora. "I told you, girls. That Gwendolyn is no friend of ours!"

*G*wennie wondered what went wrong! Could it have been a Stepella prank? Bursting into tears, she flew away crying.

$\mathcal{T}riana,$ Avalanne, and Brigitte rushed to comfort Gwendolyn. Brigitte hugged her and said, "Don't worry, Gwennie! We know you didn't make a spider dress. I would still be honored if you'd design my dress for the show."

"I would too!" said Avalanne. Gwennie wiped her tears and asked, "Really?" Triana said, "Me too! And the show is starting soon!" Gwendolyn sniffled, "I'll get your dresses and meet you on stage!"

Entering her dressing room, Gwennie heard a THUD in the closet. "What could that be?" she wondered. "All that's in there are my gown designs!"

When she opened the closet, she saw . . . "Babette?!" Gwennie gasped. Babette was stuck in some sandy muck in the closet, struggling with all of her fairy might. "I'm stuck! And my wand has been sucked down. Help!" Babette yelped.

Gwendolyn didn't stop to wonder why Babette was there, or why her closet was suddenly a quicksand pit. She grabbed Babette's hand and pulled, flapping her wings to save the meanie.

27

As Gwennie pulled Babette out of the quicksand, a jar full of spiders fell out of Babette's portfolio! "YOU put spiders on Kimora's gown!" Gwennie gasped, "Why?"

Babette said sheepishly, "I was a bit jealous of you. I was afraid the fairies would like you instead of me." Gwendolyn answered, "But Babette, you know that fairies can like both of us!"

"So you're not going to help me now, huh?" Babette frowned. "Of course I'll help you," Gwendolyn said as she gave a huge tug! Babette tumbled across the room, free from the quicksand!

"*I'm* sorry, Gwennie," Babette said, shaking sand from her wings. "I shouldn't have been such a meanie." "I forgive you," Gwennie said, looking kindly into Babette's eyes. "But wait, how did you get trapped in quicksand in my dress design closet?"

"*Oh*, um, that," Babette laughed uncomfortably. "I was in your closet doing a Sinking Sand spell to sink your gowns. It's awful! I'm so sorry! I'll tell the fairies that I was behind the spider trick!"

"*Thanks*, Babette," Gwendolyn said. "Now let's just start fresh!"

"*And* I thought it was a Stepella prank!" Gwendolyn giggled. "But for now we have a Fairy Fashion Show to put on!" The friends flew to do final styling on the hair and gowns.

Divas' Win...

*T*he Fashion Show was a crazical success! The fairies clapped most for Gwendolyn's dazzling gowns, and the special one she made for Babette. All the fairies sang,

"We want fairy dresses
just like Gwendolyn's!"

Fashion
Show

*Fashion by
Gwendolyn*

At the end of the show, Twinkle LaWinkle came to the runway and said, "I have a big announcement!" The crowd hushed. "Queen Sirona has asked me to watch for fairies who have the kind, giving heart that's required of a Real Tooth Fairy. It's the highest honor to wear the Royal Heartwing, and today I'm proud to announce . . .

"The next Real Tooth Fairy!" Everyone said, "Oo! Ahh!"

Twinkle waved her wand and an elegant package with dancing ribbons appeared.

POOF!
The box burst open to show fairy Glow, a Royal Decree and jeweled Heartwings!

Queen Sirona read the decree: "I am here to invite a fairy into the Royal Order of the Real Tooth Fairies! She has proven she has a kind and giving fairy heart, a Heart with Wings!"

"Twinkle will crown you, Gwendolyn, with the Royal Heartwing! You've shown us all how to be a beauty inside!"

Twinkle turned to a surprised Gwendolyn, "I saw the dress you secretly made for Ashley, the Earthie girl. You thought of her when you were so sad yourself! And I saw your forgiving heart today. We're honored to have you as a Real Tooth Fairy!"

"*I* will LOVE being a Real Tooth Fairy!" Gwendolyn exclaimed.

*S*he Glowed as her new friends cheered and sang:
"We want fairy hearts Just like Gwendolyn!"

The End

Twinkle is graduating from Real Fairyversity but she doesn't know what kind of fairy to be. After getting lost on Earth, will she find her true destiny?

Avalanne Fairy cheers her friends on to reach their dreams. But when her friends aren't there for her, will she give up on her own dream?

Triana Fairy has always loved helping Furries in Real Fairyland. But on an Earthie field trip, can she help some Earthie animals in imminent danger?

Gwendolyn says, "Check out the Real Fairyland books to discover the fabberful stories of how we became The Real Tooth Fairies!"

This book belongs to

whose Real Tooth Fairy is

A Real Fairytale now revealed to Earthies
By Royal Decree of Real Fairyland's Queen Sirona

Royal Council
of the
Official Seal

Love is Magic

Real Fairyland®

Published by Royal Council of the Real Fairyland, LLC
On the seaside Acorn Trail leading to the ancient fairy portal of Airlie
Wilmington, North Carolina

www.TheRealToothFairies.com

First Edition, September 2010   Printed in China
Library of Congress Cataloging-in-Publication Data
Frankel, Rachel E.
Gwendolyn Becomes a Real Tooth Fairy, Book 4/ by Rachel E. Frankel; illustrated by A-M Basom & Kelly Grupczynski.
--1st ed. p. cm -- (The Real Tooth Fairies series)
Summary: After growing up with private tutors, Gwendolyn attends her first day of school with other fairies at Real Fairyversity,
only to discover how hard it can be as the new fairy in school. At the school fashion show, Gwendolyn has a chance to
shine, but a mean girl has other plans until Gwendolyn proves that being a beauty inside is the best design of all.

Library of Congress Control Number: 2010912161
ISBN: 978-0-9841188-4-7
[1.Tooth fairy-Fiction. 2. Fairies-Fiction. 3. Teeth-Fiction 4. Family life-Kindness-Fiction. 5. Magic-Fiction.]
Visit us at www.TheRealToothFairies.com